I0787120

50 THINGS TO KNOW
BOOK SERIES
REVIEWS FROM READERS

I recently downloaded a couple of books from this series to read over the weekend thinking I would read just one or two. However, I so loved the books that I read all the six books I had downloaded in one go and ended up downloading a few more today. Written by different authors, the books offer practical advice on how you can perform or achieve certain goals in life, which in this case is how to have a better life.

The information is simple to digest and learn from, and is incredibly useful. There are also resources listed at the end of the book that you can use to get more information.

50 Things To Know To Have A Better Life: Self-Improvement Made Easy! by Dannii Cohen

---

This book is very helpful and provides simple tips on how to improve your everyday life. I found it to be useful in improving my overall attitude.

50 Things to Know For Your Mindfulness & Meditation Journey by Nina Edmondso

---

Quick read with 50 short and easy tips for what to think about before starting to homeschool.

50 Things to Know

50 Things to Know About Getting Started with Homeschool by Amanda Walton

I really enjoyed the voice of the narrator, she speaks in a soothing tone. The book is a really great reminder of things we might have known we could do during stressful times, but forgot over the years.

-    HarmonyHawaii

50 Things to Know to Manage Your Stress: Relieve The Pressure and Return The Joy To Your Life

by Diane Whitbeck

There is so much waste in our society today. Everyone should be forced to read this book. I know I am passing it on to my family.

50 Things to Know to Downsize Your Life: How To Downsize, Organize, And Get Back to Basics

by Lisa Rusczyk Ed. D.

Great book to get you motivated and understand why you may be losing motivation. Great for that person who wants to start getting healthy, or just for you when you need motivation while having an established workout routine.

50 Things To Know To Stick With A Workout: Motivational Tips To Start The New You Today

by Sarah Hughes

50 THINGS TO KNOW ABOUT WRITING ROMANCE

Esmae Browder

50 Things to Know About Writing Romance Copyright © 2018 by CZYK Publishing LLC. All Rights Reserved.

All rights reserved. No part of this book may be reproduced in any form or by any electronic or mechanical means including information storage and retrieval systems, without permission in writing from the author. The only exception is by a reviewer, who may quote short excerpts in a review.

Cover designed by: Ivana Stamenkovic
Cover Image: https://pixabay.com/en/literature-book-bindings-page-book-3060241/

CZYK Publishing Since 2011.

50 Things to Know
Visit our website at www.50thingstoknow..com

Lock Haven, PA
All rights reserved.
ISBN: 9781723834820

50 THINGS TO KNOW ABOUT WRITING ROMANCE

BOOK DESCRIPTION

Are you interested in learning what kind of characters are needed in a romance novel? Curious about the basic plot structure of what's currently selling in the market? Are you a new writer trying to understand the process of writing and what makes a romance novel stand out?

If you answered yes to any of these questions then this book is for you...

50 Things You Never Knew About Writing Romance by Esmae Browder offers a approach for beginning writers on how to be the best romance writer they can be. Most books on romance writing tell you to just write and hope for the best. Although there's nothing wrong with that, this book offers some concrete things the new writer can use to develop their romantic tales. Based on knowledge from an experienced writer, new writers will walk away with the tools to begin developing their craft and an understanding of what their next steps should be when their romance novel is complete.

In these pages you'll discover the basics of writing a hot romance that captures a reader's attention. This book will help you craft characters who feel believable and take your romance writing to the next level.

By the time you finish this book, you will know what it takes to create a successful romance novel and the next steps new writers will want to take on the road to publication. So grab YOUR copy today. You'll be glad you did.

TABLE OF CONTENTS

DEDICATION

This book is for all the new romance writers out there. Long live romance!

50 Things to Know

ABOUT THE AUTHOR

Esmae Browder is the author of the Witches of Shakespeare series and the paranormal romance, Bite Thy Neighbor. Currently located in Austin, Texas, she is always looking for ways to help other writers appreciate the craft of writing romance. A member of Romance Writers of America, you can find more information about Esmae at www.esmaebrowder.com.

Reach out to her via Facebook and Twitter.

Twitter: https://twitter.com/esmaebrowder

Facebook: https://www.facebook.com/Esmae-Browder-325152790965304/

Amazon Author Central Page: https://www.amazon.com/Esmae-Browder/e/B00M684JOC/ref=sr_ntt_srch_lnk_1?qid=1536508336&sr=8-1

INTRODUCTION

I don't think you can write - at least not well - if you don't love stories, love the written word.—
Nora Roberts

Romance—it's one of those beautiful things that wraps you in a lovely, warm embrace and leaves you thinking about the one you love long after they've gone. With all it's wonderful ups and downs, no wonder the romance genre continues to be one of the top sellers for book readers all over the world. Where else but a romance book can you forget about your own cares and worries and lose yourself for a few hours in another time and place?

Romance novels have been around much longer than most people think. Shakespeare was writing *Romeo and Juliet* over four hundred years ago. Emily Bronte was exploring the agony of lost love in *Wuthering Heights* during the mid 1800's, while F. Scott Fitzgerald dazzled us with the world of Gatsby in the roaring twenties. However, the '70s and '80s really brought the genre to the forefront of supermarket displays, making them accessible to anyone standing in the line. Beatrice Small, Rosemary Rodgers, and Kathleen Woodiwiss became household names due to their smoldering romance tales with their racy book covers.

The 2000's have ushered in all kinds of new romances, but many new authors struggle with understanding the basics of the genre and what kind of romance writer they are. Genres, sex scenes, strong hero/heroines, editing, agents, and publishing houses—it's a lot think about. This book is meant to answer questions about those topics and help guide you on the path of being the writer you want to be.

1. THE ROMANCE STIGMA

When someone asks what you write, don't be surprised if they have a preconceived idea of what romance writing is. Unfortunately, romance writing still has a stigma attached to it. Many people, including writers of other genres, feel that romance must be frivolous and easy to create. . Contrary to popular opinion, it's not all about sex or females who need a man to rescue them. Romance involves creating strong characters involved in complex and believable plots rooted in every day life. Quite often the female lead rescues herself and occasionally, even the male hero. Don't be afraid to say that you write romance and why you write it. The only way to move past a stigma is to embrace it and find ways to make others understand what romance is really all about.

2. READ THE ROMANCE GENRE

Romance is one of the hottest selling genres on the market, but you can't really write a romance if you've never read one. It may seem like a no-brainer, but knowing your genre is crucial to authors who want to get a bead on what readers are expecting when they open up your book. If there is a specific subgenre of romance you are particularly interested in writing, then it will be even more important to read books that fall within that same area. Reading how other authors handle plots and character developments is an easy way to study the craft of writing without taking an expensive class or even joining a writing group.

3. GENRE? ISN'T ROMANCE JUST ONE BIG CATEGORY?

The answer to that is no! In fact, that's a big, emphatic NO! Romance stretches into many different subgenres. True, the romance is typically the focus of the story, but there are so many ways to tell that story! Paranormal romance, fantasy, erotic, contemporary, romantic suspense, LGBT, young adult romance, historical—these are just a few of the options that are out there, and each subgenre has its own set of rules for writers to follow. It bears repeating: read your genre in order to master it. We'll discuss genres in greater detail a little further on in this book.

So what are the basics of romance? The next few tips offer an explanation of just that.

4. ROMANCE TAKES PRIORITY

If you're writing romance, the romance should be a major plot point. Some stories have a romance in them, but it's not necessarily what the story it about, and that's fine for other genres. When writing a romance novel, the love match should take priority and all other subplots should affect it in some way. Even if you are writing romantic suspense, the romance should still be a major part of the story.

5. HAPPILY EVER AFTER—FOR NOW...

A romance reader expects certain things to occur by the end of the book. The conflict will be resolved, the boy will get the girl, and everyone will live happily ever after. The ending should definitively show that and allow the reader to close the book knowing that everything is okay in the world they are leaving behind. However, there is an exception. Some endings tie the resolution up with what's called a "happily ever after for now" ending. This means that there is a possibility in the next book that our hero and heroine might not be together or could face a new hardship. Endings like this are typically the gateway into series writing.

6. KNOW YOUR TROPES

Enemies to lovers, forbidden love, falling in love with your brother's best friend—these are just a few of the romantic arcs you can find in a romance. When writing romance, it's important to know your tropes. Some publishers are looking for a specific type when they select the manuscripts they want to publish. It may feel like your repeating a familiar pattern, but sometimes familiar is good, and after all, it's all about what sells! The trick to writing tropes is to keep the pattern, but put your own spin on it.

7. ALPHA MALES RULE

They're rugged. They're tough. They melt the butter on toast with a single smoldering glance. Yes, the alpha male tends to always win the day in romance. Alphas are the ones who sweep the damsel in distress off her feet all the while single handedly taking out the bad guys. They are tough when necessary, but not afraid to show they care when it counts. Be wary of making them too perfect. We'll go into the importance of character flaws a little further on.

8. BETA MALES NEED LOVE TOO

Alpha men may dominate in the romance, but don't forget about your betas—those adorable men who may not fight the bad guys with their fists, but aren't afraid to use their brains. They order others to do the dirty work while they sit back and solve the problems of the world. They long for a woman to see them for who they are. They can be a powerful sexy, protagonist who doesn't need to resort to violence to get the girl into their bed or heart.

9. DAMSELS IN DISTRESS

Even in this day and age, the damsel in distress is a thing—especially in historical romance. What is a damsel in distress? A woman in need of rescuing from the evil bad guy whoever he may be in her world. Back in the '70s and 80's when romance began to get really popular, the damsel in distress was the scantily clad woman on the cover of the romance book. Heaving bosoms, ripped bodices, and a feeling that the problems of the world just couldn't be solved by anyone but a man were the hallmarks of that style of book. While this is still true in some romances, nowadays a damsel in distress is more than capable of rescuing herself. When writing this type of character, be careful of making her a stereotype or caricature. Readers in today's world tend to want their heroines with more grit and independence. Sometimes they even save the hero.

10. AND SPEAKING OF ROMANCE COVERS...

Remember that old saying, "Never judge a book by its cover?" Like it or not, a book cover can give a great deal of information. If you are going to publish your own book, that cover can make or break the success of your novel. If your story is a sweetheart romance, but you've got a bare chested man with long flowing hair and a devil may care grin on the front cover, that could be a problem. A reader does judge what the book is about based on the cover. If they purchase something based on the look of the cover, they could feel cheated if the book doesn't deliver. No author wants a bad review because a graphic misled the audience. Make sure your cover reflects your genre.

11. MAKE YOUR COUPLE FIGHT FOR IT

Ah…sweet, sweet love. There's nothing better than having the couple who you know should be together fall in love in your story. However, it's important to be careful about when this occurs. Give your reader some conflict, something that makes the couple have to overcome an obstacle threatening to keep them apart. If they get together early in the book, that's fine. Make them blissfully happy and then take that happiness away as soon as possible so we can watch how they handle a new challenge.

12. INSTANT ATTRACTION

If there's one rule of romance to follow, it's the rule of instant attraction. Your hero and heroine should feel a spark from the moment they meet. That doesn't mean they have to fall in love at that instant. The build up to that realization is too important to be passed over so quickly, but even if they don't actually like each other, the attraction should be there. Nothing creates conflict like being attracted to the man you're supposed to hate, to the woman who stole your family's fortune, or the high school sweetheart who you just can't quite get over. Establish that spark early on and your reader will be hooked.

13. SEX OR NO SEX?

Sex or no sex—that is the question! Believe it or not, there is an art to writing a great sex scene. Some authors don't feel comfortable writing about the act itself and choose to handle the issue by having it happen "off stage" or by giving the moment a "fade to black" feel where the reader can imagine what is going on. Other authors go for the whole enchilada and write scenes that steam up your glasses in a heartbeat. What's right for you? Again, you must consider your genre and what its expectations are, as well as, thinking about what you are comfortable writing. This will determine your level of heat. A word of advice to the new writer: don't write as if your mother is looking over your shoulder. When you do that, your writing becomes stilted and unnatural. Let the words flow and worry later about what your momma might think.

14. CAN YOU SHOW HEAT WITHOUT SEX?

Sex is not the only way to show heat between a couples in a romance. A touch of the hand, tucking a strand of someone's hair behind their ear, thinking about them when their gone, a simple hug—all of these are ways to show that your characters care about each other. Our hearts fill with longing when love blossoms slowly and sometimes the best love stories are the ones where the physical intimacy is left out. We like the couple so much that we're rooting for them to kiss or admit their feelings for each other. Other ways to show heat without sex are trembling hands, mouth going dry, a warm feeling in the belly, wiping a way a tear, complimenting that love interest when they're not around, and using grand gesture.

15. BEWARE THE QUIVERING MEMBER

You've decided what kind or romance to write and know it's going to have some hot scenes. You sit down to write it and suddenly the words you are typing to describe their love seems a bit silly. This is a common problem for the romance writer. The correct clinical term for body parts may be appropriate, but can often read (pardon the pun) a little stiffly. Ask yourself some basic questions: what time period is your story in and what kind of people are your characters? Time period matters because certain slang terms commonly used to describe body parts would not have been used a hundred years ago. Using those terms in a historical will bring your reader crashing back to the present day at the most inopportune time in your book. It's also worth nothing that there are certain terms that are outdated and over used even in a historical, too. Quivering members, love nubs, and creamy white orbs should be used with caution.

As previously mentioned, reading your genre and getting a feel for what is current will help you immensely when it comes to writing a descriptive, contemporary love scene. Make a list of all phrases or terms you discover that are interesting and perhaps a different way to describe the physical attributes of a character. Refer to your list often and try to avoid using the same phrase over and over. A word of advice: The only way to get comfortable writing sex scenes is to keep writing them. Eventually, you'll get a feel for what does and doesn't work.

16. WHAT'S IN A NAME?

Character names are fun to come up with, but don't go over board. Jack and Sally are still perfectly respectable names, but so often in romance, the hero and heroine seem to have unusual names. That's fine, but don't pick names with difficult pronunciations unless you're going to provide an explanation of how to say them. Names like Siobhan and Aoife are lovely, but unless you know someone named either of those, they can also be difficult to figure out how to pronounce. Also be careful of having too many character names that start with the same beginning letter. If you have five characters named Jack, Jean, Joan, Judy, and John, it's difficult for the reader to sort out who is who. Your goal is to make things simple for the reader when it comes to names.

17. FIVE SENSES CAN STRENGTHEN YOUR STORY

Touch, sight, smell, sound, and taste are things probably first learnt back in grade school. As an author, the five senses are an important part of storytelling. They provide additional details that strengthen the setting and the story. Sensory experiences trigger memories in all of us. Describing how a character's senses affect them puts the reader in their shoes, allowing them to use their own sensory recall to relate to the situation. The five senses should be present in every scene you write whether you write romance or a different genre.

Pro tip: When you edit, one of the things on your editing checklist should be whether you've included the five senses. A great place to include many of these is when your setting the scene for each chapter. The good news is that you don't have to go over board with this. A simple word here and there will add depth to the story.

18. STRONG BACKGROUND CHARACTERS ARE IMPORTANT

The romance may take priority, but that doesn't mean you can't include quirky and fun characters who help drive the action along. A wise cracking grandma, a crazy best friend, the nice bartender who always has advice for everyone are all great characters to include in your story and they can have their own backstories and plots as long as they don't detract from the main plotline. Sometimes these characters may resonate strongly with you as an author and be a stepping-stone to writing the next book.

If you find that particular characters keep drawing your attention, make notes about them. Flesh out some ideas regarding how they could have their own romance or own stand alone tale in a different book. Who are they? What makes them tick? These are details you don't need to include in the current manuscript you're writing, but they may come in handy later on.

19. WATCH OUT FOR TOO MUCH BACK STORY

Of course you're reader wants to know the history of your characters. Where they come from and what traumatic experience has made them the way they are is important information, making them feel much more three dimensional. Yet, too much back story stops the forward action and slows down the story. It may not be necessary to explain every nuance of their childhood or exactly how they're related to their first cousin once removed. That doesn't mean you shouldn't know those things as the writer, and If it somehow develops the plot, great. Otherwise, less is more. Along those lines, back story doesn't have to spill out at the beginning of the book. Give the reader just a little at a time and save the good stuff for later in the story when your reader is really hooked.

As a beginning writer, how do you know you have too much backstory? Lots of flashbacks, constant mentions of the past, a feeling that the plot is going nowhere fast—these are good ways to tell if you need to make cuts. Flashbacks have their place and can be a good tool to deliver information, but many agents and editors are turned off by that writing device. See if you can find other ways to provide character history.

20. THE SCENE WHERE IT ALL FALLS APART

Your characters are attracted to each other. They spend most of their time together, and even more time thinking about each other when they're apart. Laughter, glances full of longing, kisses—it's all been experienced and happily ever after is within reach. However tempting it may be to let the love flow freely, your reader wants more. You need the moment where it all falls apart—the moment when their happiness is lost and it looks like nothing will ever be right again. This goes back to the idea previously mentioned of making your couple fight for their relationship. The moment of crisis is important. It puts their love to the test and proves whether or not they're meant to be together. Don't skip this important scene.

This scene is where character flaws come in handy. We don't want any character to be too perfect and in this big scene, we need to see it all on display. Jealousy, a misunderstanding, the long over due argument—create a situation that can't be easily solved right away. Let your characters feel the full weight of misery so they can realize how much they can't live without each other.

21. REDEEMABLE HEROES

This ties into the idea of character flaws. Don't make your hero or heroine perfect. We won't a realistic character with flaws that can be forgiven or fixed at some point. No one is perfect. Let us see that in your romantic male lead. What tortures them? What keeps them awake at night? Why do they feel that nothing can be right for them ever again? Make them a character of fictional flesh and blood the reader can root for.

22. THAT SCENE WHERE IT ALL COMES BACK TOGETHER

Just as crucial to the story is the scene where it all gets resolved. As a reader, we've been with your characters every step of the way. We've hurt for them, ached for them, cried tears of frustration at their pitfalls, and now Dear Author, we are counting on you to make all the wrongs right. Your hero and heroine need to come to big revelations that change them in some way and furthers the action. This is the moment of apology, the moment of forgiveness, the moment the characters truly know they can't live without each other. Don't leave us hanging. We deserve our happily ever after.

That being said, the minor characters in your story may not always get a clear resolution to their stories. In fact, some of the things that happen to them may be the set up for your next book if you are writing a series. For example, the quirky best friend of the hero never seems lucky in love, and once again, he strikes out in this story. However, he might turn out to be the romantic hero in the next book who falls in love with his dream girl and gets his own sweet ending.

23. MARRIAGE?

Marriage is often the endgame in a romance, but most publishers don't want to see contemporary stories where a married couple is the focus. Yes, marriages have their share of romance and wonderful times, but stories where the married couple cheat on each other is not romantic. There are always exceptions to the rule, (think Nora Roberts In Death series) but most romances are about bringing a couple together whether it's a happily ever after or a happily ever after for now.

Some times in a historical romance, marriages of convenience are used. The couple in question doesn't want to be married but have no say in the matter. Finding ways to make them fall in love after the fact can be fun. Just remember that if they are already married or get married during the story, be sure to provide some conflict so your reader can root for them to overcome their obstacles.

24. HOW DO I KNOW MY GENRE?

As promised, we have come back to the topic of genre. If you are just starting to write romance, you may be uncertain what category your manuscript falls into. Don't assume an agent or editor will sort it out for you. Most of them expect you to know what genre you're writing in prior to receiving your submission. If you are uncertain, ask yourself the following questions. What style feels right to you? When you think about your story and characters what do you think of? Are you drawn to the past? Firmly rooted in the present? Or do you like hot werewolves with bulging biceps? Write what comes easiest to start with and don't worry about what anyone else thinks. It's possible that you may enjoy writing more than one genre and there's nothing wrong with that. For a better explanation of just a few of the romance genres, read on!

25. CONTEMPORARY FUN

As the title implies, contemporary romance is happening right now in this time period. It's full of modern, every day language and situations. The setting is a familiar location whether it's a small town or a big city of note. The girl and the guy meet in some fun manner and the attraction is instant—even if they think they hate each other. There is a conflict of some sort, but at the end of it all they are emotionally laid bare and discover just how right they are for each other. The ending is either a HEA or a HEA for now. This popular category generally can have it's own subcategories and can have varying levels of heat. There are lots of subgenres in this category so do your research to see where your work fits.

26. HISTORICAL LOVE RULES THE REGENCY

Ah…the historical romance…so juicy, so gossipy, and so rife with bodice-laced passion that you can't even handle it. Historical romance also has many sub-genres within it and includes a variety of time periods such as Viking, Middle Ages, Tudor, Victorian England, Civil War, and western. Regency romance (late 1800's-early 1900's) continues to be a popular genre within the historical romance market and often includes steamy and descriptive love scenes.

27. WEREWOLVES, VAMPIRES, AND WITCHES: OH MY!

The paranormal romance genre has its ebb and flow in the romance market. While werewolves and vampires may flit in an out of popularity, they never go away for good. This genre is full of magic and things that go bump in the night. It allows for the impossible to be possible and provides a nice range of romantic possibilities in varying heat levels.

28. A TALE OF EROTIC ROMANCE

Erotic romance is usually heavy with sexual tension and descriptive sexual scenes. However, that doesn't mean it's considered a porn story. What distinguishes this category is that the sex is what drives the story forward. Don't write a sex scene without purpose. Once the sex is over one or more of the characters involved should be changed in some way, thus furthering the action. This is also a category that sometimes is woven within other genres, too.

29. SWEETS TO THE SWEET

Sweetheart romance is a subgenre of contemporary romance, but is so popular it rates a separate mention. Sweetheart is character driven with a focus on the romance being a major plot point. Unlike other categories of romance, sex does not happen on the page. It's either behind closed doors or not happening at all. That doesn't mean there is no heat between your characters, but it is expressed in a less overtly sexual way.

30. WHAT COMES NEXT?

You've written your romance. It's hot and ready to go. Or so you think…if this is the first draft of your book, it's a good idea to let it rest for a while and then go over it again. You want to find all the typos and the grammatical errors. Fix them and then re-read the manuscript. Does it flow? Are your characters strong and believable? Are there plot holes in the story? Do your romance characters spend the majority of their time on the page together or at least thinking about each other? Most authors don't write the perfect manuscript on the first try, and regardless of genre, it's common to create several drafts of the story. Don't rush this process. Editing may be tedious, but this is where the fine-tuning to your creation happens. Polish the manuscript within in inch of its life before even thinking about submitting it to an agent, publisher, or self-publishing.

31. TO AGENT OR NOT TO AGENT

Romance writers, as well as authors who write in other genres, often ponder the value of getting an agent. There was a time when not having an agent was unthinkable if you were considering publication. In the last decade, the path to publication has broadened and agents are not always needed in order for an author to get their work in front of a reader. Self-publishing has opened the door for writers to take control of every aspect of their career. However, that path is not always viable for everyone and takes a lot of work. This is where having an agent would come in handy. An agent's job is to help an author get their manuscript in the best possible shape and then get it read by an editor or publisher who works with a publishing house. They negotiate all kinds of options in a publishing contract including things like overseas rights or movie rights and get a percentage of whatever price is agreed upon by the publisher of your book. All in all, an agent can get you a better deal than most people can get on their own and are more apt to get the book in front of a larger publishing house.

32. SMALL PRESS PUBLISHERS

A romance author has many options when it comes to publishing. If you choose not to get an agent or are having trouble getting one, consider submitting your work to a small press. Small presses provide many of the same options that a larger publishing house does—just on a smaller scale. You generally don't need an agent to submit to a small press, but you will sign a contract with them. Read it over carefully and make sure you understand the terms. Small presses of merit will provide an editor for you, cover art, and help you promote your eBook. Your book may not necessarily be available in a brick and mortar bookstore, but POD (print on demand) is usually available, which means a physical copy of your book can be ordered for purchase. However, some presses do not provide that option. Be sure to check your contract carefully if that is important to you.

Research your small press to make sure it publishes your genre of romance and find out how much you get paid per book sold. While most presses will help with advertising, a large part of it will fall on the author's shoulders. This can be time consuming and expensive.

33. SELF PUBLISHING

Self publishing used to be a dirty word. People who self published were authors who couldn't write well and had nothing to offer. That wasn't true then and it's certainly not true now! Self-publishing has caught on, and with big platforms like Amazon to work with, the sky is the limit for authors. When it comes to self publishing, a writer needs to do their research. Book covers, editing, and marketing—it will all fall to the author to take care of those things. While some may find that liberating, others may find it discouraging and costly. This style of publishing requires patience and the ability to multi-task as both a creative mind and business mind.

It's important to note, that while there are some fabulous success stories out there regarding authors who have made the big time by self publishing, those stories are few and far between. The competition to stand out is fierce and waiting a long time between publications can cause readers to lose interest. This feeling of urgency causes many writers to produce work that has been poorly edited or not edited at all. Please don't let fall into that trap. Hire an editor if you have to and publish the best version of your work you can.

34. PUTTING YOURSELF OUT THERE

No matter what publishing path you take, they will have to do some marketing. In the 80's and '90's, marketing was something that fell on the shoulders of the publishers marketing team. With the advent of the Internet, that is no longer the case. Yes, big publishing companies still do lots of promotions for a title, but it is expected that the author will help promote their book. Be prepared to have a website, a newsletter, and various social media accounts. All of these things drive business to your work and help readers get to know you. Making friends with other members of the romance writing community is a great idea, too. Writing can be a lonely business so supporting others with the same interest is a win-win, not just for book sales, but also for your own sanity. If you're an introvert, this will be hard, but the pay off can be worth it.

35. STAND ALONE OR SERIES

Is your book a stand alone or is there series potential? Series tend to be a big hit with romance readers. Remember those fun, quirky minor characters you created in book one? A series allows you to take those characters and go a step further. Readers love to revisit familiar locations and learn about what's been happening in that world. Series can also translate into bigger sales as more fans discover your series.

If you are uncertain that you have the stamina to write a series, try plotting one out. Create a brief synopsis of the ideas you have for other characters and see where it leads. Write a rough draft for the next book in your series and then let it sit while you concentrate on writing something else.

36. SHOULD I GET A CRITIQUE PARTNER?

The decision to share your work with a beta reader or a critique partner is a personal one. Some authors find the feedback, suggestions, and advice they receive from a writer friend or a critique group invaluable. Others feel it stifles their own creativity. As mentioned before, writing can be a lonely business with few people around who understand how hard it is to craft a great story or to cut that same great story down to a manageable plot line. A critique partner can be helpful on those days when you need to vent or talk about how the work is going. They can provide wisdom and help you see things in a different way. When choosing a partner, look for someone whose advice you value and trust.

37. MY NAME OR SOMETHING ELSE?

Some authors decide to publish under a name that is not their given name. There are lots of reasons they choose to do this. Maybe they are uncomfortable with the people in the church congregation knowing they write steamy sex scenes. Perhaps they work in education and want to protect young minds from things they may not be ready for. Or it could simply be that the author has been writing in a different genre and doesn't want to confuse his/her readers. Having a pen name can be a great tool to develop creativity as there is a certain freedom in anonymity. However, if you already write under your given name and have a social media following, you'll need to create a separate account for you non de plume. That means two websites, two of each social media account, and so on. Keeping up with two of everything can be challenging so think long and hard about whether or not creating a pen name is right for you. Many authors opt not to hide the fact that they write under a pen name at all. Instead, they have a separate section on their webpage that indicates their other persona and style of books.

38. THE SYNOPSIS IS YOUR FRIEND

If you've ever had to write a synopsis for a manuscript, you already know how challenging it can be to condense into a short blurb or even a few pages the entire story. Many writers think that writing the synopsis should occur once the manuscript is finished. However, some find that writing a synopsis prior to starting the manuscript keeps them on track. Laying out the finer plot points allows the author to develop story lines as needed while still keeping the end in mind. The synopsis can also be an easy character cheat sheet that lets the writer keep straight the character names, eye color, hair color, and relationships to each other.

The synopsis will need to written though. When you submit your manuscript, including a short synopsis is typically a requirement. Why? It gives the person considering your work an overview of the story, but also of your writing style. Parts of you synopsis can also be used later on when it comes writing the blurb for the back of your book, too.

39. CUT UNNECESSARY WORDS

Way back in middle school we were taught that words ending in "ly" were important, and while they can add description to a tale, use them with care. Sometimes these words are fluff and your manuscript can be just as strong without them. Cutting words and phrases help you to tighten the story and can help reduce the word count. There are many resources that can assist you in this process such as The Elements of Style by William Strunk or The Chicago Manual of Style.

40. THE DREADED QUERY LETTER

If you think writing the synopsis is hard, try writing the query letter. Cutting your work down to two-three paragraphs in a letter is a challenge. How do you convey the highlights of your story without telling everything? It's tough, but you can do it. Please keep in mind that the query letter is extremely important. It's the first contact you will have with the person who could potentially be your agent or editor. You want to hook them in the first paragraph by writing a great opening line that gets their attention. That first paragraph should quickly introduce one of your characters and set up what their problem is. Paragraph two introduces the second character and how he/she can help or hinder the problem. Paragraph three is about the obstacle they face. Paragraph four is where you give the title, word count, genre, what you've written, and that you are looking to be published or represented.

A good query letter takes time to be crafted. Don't rush it and have someone else read it over before you send it. Does it hook them? Make them want to read more?

41. EDIT, EDIT, AND EDIT SOME MORE

Let's talk a little more about editing. When you edit, you want to take care of those grammatical errors such as spelling mistakes, comma's, periods, etc. Those are basics though. Editing is more than just looking for those basic things. It's about cutting unnecessary words and dialogue tags. This is the time to trim scenes and make them more coherent. Characters grow stronger, more vivid during the editing process. Keep notes of different ideas you have and incorporate them into the story without adding back story which can slow the flow of the plot. Realize this: editing is not a one time thing. It's a continual process that may take up many drafts of the story until you feel it's complete.

42. REALISTIC DIALOGUE

Dialogue can be quite a challenge. Creating dialogue that moves the reader and sounds real is even tougher. In every day life, the words we say and the rhythm we speak them are all natural and not something most people give much thought to. As a romance writer, you have to make your characters talk to each other in a way that seems natural for their time and situation. What sounds good in your head, doesn't always read well on the page. While we may say "um…" quite often in real life, using that particular word on the page detracts from what is being said. One way to help with this is to read your dialogue out loud. Something about hearing the words spoken triggers the brain to recognize what sounds real and what is forced.

43. TAKE A CLASS

Education doesn't stop just because you graduate from school. Romance authors are always learning, always finding ways to take their writing to the next level. If you are uncertain about how to strengthen your manuscript, find a class in your area that offers some guidance. Reach out to local writing groups and see what kind of offerings they have. A class environment is great way to hone in on specific areas that you need help with and can connect you with other writers who write in the same genre.

44. ROMANCE REVIEWS

Once you've published your book by either traditional or non-traditional means, the next step can be a nailbiter. That first manuscript is like a new born baby. You've worked and slaved over it. Now it's time to let it go and the reviews are going to come in. Hopefully, they will all be positive, well-written reviews that do nothing but bring attention to your book. However, it's possible you might receive some negative feedback, too. As tempting as it is to respond to it, don't. Let it go and remember that it's just one person's opinion. Many writers don't even read their reviews at all! So what are you supposed to do instead of seeing what people are saying about your book? Start writing the next one.

45. ROMANCE REJECTION

There will come a point when you lean back from your computer and say, "Finished." That's the time when you know you're ready to share the romance with the world. This might mean starting on the road to self publication or maybe you will begin the process of submitting your work to an agent or publishing house. If you choose to go the submission process route, read the guidelines on your prospective agent or publishing houses' website. They often list exactly what they are looking for and how you should submit the story. Some will want just a short query letter and synopsis. Others will want those things and your full manuscript. Most likely they will ask you to submit those things electronically.

After you hit the send button for submissions, then the waiting begins. It is common to wait 4-6 weeks before you hear a response about your works, and in some cases, it can be months. If you get a rejection, don't lose heart. Keep submitting! What doesn't work for one person, may work for another. If you are lucky enough to get a rejection with any kind of notes regarding your submission, pay attention. There's something specific there that you can hone in on and rework—especially if you keep getting the same note over and over. The important thing to remember is not to give up. Keep submitting, and while you're waiting for that acceptance letter, write the next book.

46. SETTINGS MATTER

When you write your manuscript, keep in mind the setting or location of the story. It does matter. Some locations lend themselves easier to romance than others, but some readers are looking for specific romances that take place in certain locations. For instance, small town romances with quirky town characters that remind one of television shows like Gilmore Girls or Hart of Dixie are popular with lots of readers. The big city where the hero is a billionaire always in control of his world until the pretty nobody heroine disrupts it is another common setting device. Regency romance is typically set in England, allowing for old customs and gorgeous gowns to be on full display. Summer romances, Christmas affairs with snowy locations, and mountain ranges with outdoorsy themes all lend themselves to romantic settings. Make the setting a third character and you've added richness to the tapestry of your story.

47. FOLLOW THE TRENDS

When writing romance, it is important to look at the trends. What is currently selling in the field of romance? Some authors reject the idea that they should be writing a story based on a formula or trend, but there is something to be said for studying what readers want and what publishers are selecting to represent. Showing that you can write what's hot on the market is an excellent way to get your foot in the door, and once you've established yourself, then you can write that off the beaten path novel you've been secretly working on. Ideally, you want to write whatever kind of romance is popular and then put your own spin on it in order to stand out.

48. HEAD HOPPING IS A NO NO

Ever read a book and found yourself wondering who is talking or whose thoughts you are reading? When the thought process of characters is switching back and forth constantly within a chapter, that's called head hopping. Head hopping can be used effectively, but it's typically frowned on as it confuses the reader. If you are a beginning writer, please don't head hop. Stay in one character's point of view until the next chapter. That doesn't mean you can't have both hero and heroine on the same page. In fact, they should be spending as much time together as possible. Keeping each chapter in one character's point of view allows us to see what they think about the other person and learn whom they really are. In a romance, this helps us understand what attracts them to each other and provides insights on the things they do that are known or unknown to further the romance.

49. THE DAILY WORD COUNT

Word counts can be the bane of your existence as a writer or the thing that gets you through the next chapter. Setting a daily goal of how much you are going to write is a good idea. When you are writing your first draft, don't worry about spelling or editing. Just write and hit the your word count. There will be plenty of time to go back later and add detail or correct those glaring grammatical errors.

50. SCHEDULE YOUR TIME

A common question asked of writers is, "how you do manage your writing time?" Many writers have families and day jobs that take up a large portion of their day. When do they find the time to write? Some do it early in the morning, others late at night. It's all about finding what works best for you. Maybe you're in a position where you can only write on the weekends. There is no wrong or right way to be a writer. That being said, if you want to make a career out of writing while balancing all the other things going on in your life, you will need to come up with some sort of schedule and stick to it. This is where having a daily work count goal or weekly goal comes in handy. Be sure to tell your loved ones when your writing time is and that you need them to give you that time without interruption. This can be hard at first, but once you establish a routine, everyone will fall into your groove.

50 Things to Know

OTHER HELPFUL RESOURCES

Romance writers have lots of places they can research this topic further. Listed here are a few great resources.

Romance Writers of America https://www.rwa.org/

Goodreads
https://www.goodreads.com/

Avon Romance
https://www.feedspot.com/infiniterss.php?q=site:http%3A%2F%2Fwww.avonromance.com%2Ffeed

Harlequin
https://www.harlequin.com/shop/index.html

50 Things to Know

READ OTHER

50 THINGS TO KNOW

BOOKS

50 Things to Know to Get Things Done Fast: Easy Tips for Success

50 Things to Know About Going Green: Simple Changes to Start Today

50 Things to Know to Live a Happy Life Series

50 Things to Know to Organize Your Life: A Quick Start Guide to Declutter, Organize, and Live Simply

50 Things to Know About Being a Minimalist: Downsize, Organize, and Live Your Life

50 Things to Know About Speed Cleaning: How to Tidy Your Home in Minutes

50 Things to Know About Choosing the Right Path in Life

50 Things to Know to Get Rid of Clutter in Your Life: Evaluate, Purge, and Enjoy Living

50 Things to Know About Journal Writing: Exploring Your Innermost Thoughts & Feelings

50 Things to Know

Website: 50thingstoknow.com

Facebook: facebook.com/50thingstoknow

Pinterest: pinterest.com/lbrennec

YouTube: youtube.com/user/50ThingsToKnow

Twitter: twitter.com/50ttk

Mailing List: Join the 50 Things to Know
Mailing List to Learn About New Releases

50 Things to Know

50 Things to Know

Please leave your honest review of this book on Amazon and Goodreads. We appreciate your positive and constructive feedback. Thank you.

www.ingramcontent.com/pod-product-compliance
Lightning Source LLC
Chambersburg PA
CBHW031324250726
48656CB00005B/1960